The Twilight Marsh

The Twilight Marsh

And Other Wilderness Adventures

TODD LEE

POLESTAR
BOOK PUBLISHERS

Published by
Polestar Press Ltd.
1011 Commercial Drive, Second Floor
Vancouver, B.C.
Canada   V5L 3X1

The publisher would like to thank the Canada Council, the British Columbia Ministry of Small Business, Tourism and Culture, and the Department of Canadian Heritage for their ongoing financial assistance.

Cover illustration and design, and interior illustrations by Jim Brennan
Interior design and production by Sandra Robinson
Printed in Canada by Best Book Manufacturers

Canadian Cataloguing in Publication Data

Lee, Todd, 1924-
The twilight marsh, and other wilderness adventures

ISBN 1-896095-07-0

1. British Columbia, Northern—Juvenile fiction. 2. Children's stories, Canadian (English) * I. Title.
PS8573.E3532T94 1995   jC813'.54   C95-910193-4
PZ7.L43Tw 1995

Contents

This book is dedicated to the memory of my daughter,
Patricia Anne Lee.

A Cry in the Night

EEU...WAUGH...EEEUGH!

My arms half-loaded with firewood, I froze in my tracks, wondering if that terrible scream would be repeated, hoping that it would not come again. Bob stood, axe in his hand, as startled as I was.

Late in doing chores, we had gone to the woodshed in early dark to haul in wood for the evening. Made friendly by the call of nighthawks and chirping of pine beetles, the dark was something we were seldom afraid of. Now, the trees pressing close around the ranch buildings seemed drenched in suspense and fear, fear of what we could not see!

AGH...EEEEEE...AWOUGH!

This time, fear gave wings to our feet. Throwing down wood and axe, we fled to the safety of the house.

"Mom, Mom!" Bob shouted.

Mom met us on the back porch. One look at her face told us that she had also heard.

"Mom, what is it?" I gasped. We stared hard into the dusk, looking across the creek where the rambling pasture fence lost itself in shadows.

"I...I don't know, Gary!" Mom answered through tight lips. "I've never heard anything like it before."

We had moved from a small farm in California to this wilderness cattle ranch in British Columbia, miles from our nearest neighbour. There were many things to learn, such as the identity of this terrible shriek in the night. Maybe Dad would know, but he had gone by saddle horse to get our mail.

"Maybe it's a *cougar*!" I whispered hoarsely. Shortly after we arrived on the ranch, neighbour John Hailie had warned Mom and Dad not to let us go into the woods alone in case a cougar attacked us. Other neighbours laughed at this. They had never seen a cougar in this area. Yet, surely it would have to be something big and fierce to make a noise like that!

The scream came again and was followed by the drum

*I froze in my tracks, wondering if that terrible scream
would be repeated...*

of hooves. Bob and I retreated to the open door. Our mother stood alone, tense and uncertain.

"The horses!" Bob cried out. "Something must be after our horses! Mom, we've got to do *something*!"

"If only your father were here!" Mom exclaimed. "He would know what kind of danger this is. Whatever can be keeping him this late?"

One of the horses, Nancy probably, whinnied. The sound, high-pitched and shrill, seemed to be filled with terror. Again there was a thunder of hooves. That would be Caesar, our big Percheron stallion. Could Caesar protect our horses from a cougar? I trembled at the thought of such a contest.

"Bob, did Dad take the rifle with him? Run and see!" Mom directed.

"I don't think so!" Bob ran to the living room where the rifle rested on a set of moose antlers. In a moment he was back, staggering under the weight of the hunting rifle.

"Here it is!" Bob announced. "Oh, I forgot the shells. They're in the closet, aren't they, Mom?" He was back in a minute, a clip of rifle shells clutched in his hands.

Mom levered a shell into the barrel of the rifle, being careful to point it away from the house. She had never fired a rifle this big before, but it took her only moments to puzzle it out.

"But I don't see anything to shoot at!" Mom protested. "Whatever it is, it's out there in the dark. I can't shoot what I can't see!"

It was true. Our fear had been so real we could picture teeth and claws on every movement in the shadows. As yet, there was nothing to indicate that the fearful beast, whatever it was, had come into the barnyard.

"Maybe it's gone away..." I began hopefully, then stopped with a gasp.

EEEEEEE...AWHOOOO...EEEEEEE!

Whatever was making that fearful cry was still out there in the dark. The horses were racing about now, milling around in the barnyard. We could hear snorts and grunts and a clatter against the rickety fence. Mom held the rifle in front of her, straining to see through the night.

"Mom!" I cried out. "You've got to do something! Poor Caesar—he might be killed!"

With lips pressed tight, Mom pointed the rifle at the ragged line where forest met sky, and pulled the trigger. There was a frightful crash and flame spurted from the barrel. Echoes bounced back and forth from hill to hill.

We heard the horses race to the end of the barnyard and Caesar's snort of alarm. At the same time we heard the pounding of hooves from the other direction. A rider came around the corner of the house—Dad!

"Hey, what's going on around here? I heard a shot!"

"Thank goodness you're back!" Mom gasped, letting the rifle butt slip to the porch. "We've just heard the most frightful cry!"

It came again! A gurgling, strangled cry, more terrifying than before. In the stunned silence that followed, we gazed at Dad, wondering what he would do. To our surprise, he broke into a grin.

"Is that what you were afraid of?" he asked, smiling.

We nodded dumbly. Seeing his grin, we were reluctant to voice our fears.

"You really don't know?" Dad could see from our serious expressions that we didn't know what it was. "Well, I guess you wouldn't have heard it before."

Then Dad explained. A herd of wild horses, led by a mustang stallion, had drifted in from Burnt Mountain Range. It was Caesar, challenging, and the mustang replying that had made those frightful screams!

So that was it. Now Bob and I could understand the sound of running hooves and the exciting whinnying. It was our turn to grin—with relief! But we would never forget our terror that night when we heard such a frightful scream—the cry of a wild mustang!

Mystery of the Twilight Marsh

"DAD, THIS CREEK IS JUST A swamp!" Bob said with disgust. "Let's go back and explore the lake. That will be more fun."

"No, Bob," Dad answered. "A swamp can be an exciting place to explore, especially in the evening. Just sit quietly. Watch and listen."

We were in our old sixteen-foot canoe. Dad paddled in the stern, while Bob was the bow paddler. Being the lightest, I sat on the middle seat. Even though I didn't say anything, in my heart I agreed with Bob. The creek was full of weeds and had a foul smell of decaying water lily roots.

In the mouth of the creek a heavy growth of water lily pads blocked the way, but our canoe passed easily over them. High, rank swamp grass closed us in on either side.

For a few minutes nothing moved and we heard nothing but the soft splash of the paddle blades. Then there was a rustling in the grass to our right, and two "plops" in the water. I opened my mouth to comment, but Dad held up a warning finger for silence.

Suddenly two furry heads with bright and curious eyes popped to the surface. Both animals uttered sharp snorts and hisses. I turned back to Dad with unspoken questions.

"Otters," Dad whispered. "Don't move!"

In one motion the heads were replaced by long furry tails as the otters up-ended and disappeared. Moments later they appeared on the other side of the canoe. The whistling snorts were repeated, this time with a challenge. They viewed us with suspicion, their bristling whiskers twitching.

As if a signal had passed between them, they began to play, chasing each other in circles above and below the surface. Sometimes they were on one side of the canoe, sometimes on the other. Their loud snorts and whistles continued.

Bob chuckled out loud and at once the furry clowns disappeared. For some time we could hear them following along through the rank swamp grass, snorting and blowing.

"They may have young ones somewhere close," Dad explained. "All these antics could have been to divert our attention and lead us away. Still bored?"

"No way!" I replied excitedly. "That was neat."

More adventure lay just around the next bend where an old beaver dam had widened the creek. A mother mallard duck swam away from us followed by six ducklings in single file.

"Look!" Bob exclaimed.

Startled, mother duck began a great flapping in the water as though she were badly injured. As we drew closer, her antics increased, accompanied by shrill quacks.

"Say, where are the ducklings?" I asked, peering around on both sides of the canoe.

"They're safely hidden under lily pads, or in the grass," Dad replied. "All that frantic flapping was just to divert our attention while the babies hid."

We had to stop and slide the canoe over the next beaver dam. For some time we paddled along, making no sound except for the whispering of lily pads against our keel. I was really intent now, alert for new things to see.

Suddenly there was a loud SPLAT! Just ahead of us the water boiled while a circle of ripples spread out across the creek. I could see a broad wake as something swam under water to the left bank.

"Did you see what that was?" I called softly to Bob in the front of the canoe.

"A beaver, I think," Bob whispered back.

"You're right, Bob. He slapped the water with his tail to warn other beavers. Just keep still; his curiosity will bring him back," Dad cautioned.

He was right. A moment later a large brown head broke water and cruised around our canoe, almost within paddle reach. I'm sure he was as curious as we were. When Bob lifted his paddle, the beaver dived again, bringing his broad, flat tail down to make a resounding report.

"See that hump of branches and mud over there in the grass?" Dad pointed with his paddle. "That's the beaver colony house. Probably there are young beaver in there and father beaver is standing guard."

"How come there isn't a dam?" Bob wanted to know. "I thought beavers always built a dam near their house."

"Not always," Dad said. "They build dams to raise the water high enough to protect the entrances to their house. Here the creek is deep enough so they don't have to build. See, there's water all around their house and into the bushes where they bring in their food."

"I don't see where they enter the house," I put in, trying to see into the creek bed nearest to the beaver's house.

"Oh, you won't see the entrance anywhere near the house. It starts well away, near the bottom, and comes up directly under the house. That will fool their enemies."

"Look there!"

Another furry head popped to the surface some twenty feet from the point where the colony house stood.

"That is probably where the entry tunnel is," Dad explained.

"They must be very clever animals," Bob replied.

*They viewed us with suspicion, their bristling
whiskers twitching.*

17

"Right up with the best of them," Dad answered. "For instance, we don't know how they can take a floating poplar log to the bottom of the pond and manage to keep it there for winter food."

We had not paddled far when we saw another native of the swamp. A muskrat swam out from the bank leaving a sharp vee in the water as it turned away from us. I noticed something different about it.

"Look!" I called out. "One of her babies is riding on her back. It must be moving day."

"What happens when the mother goes under water," Bob asked.

"It will hang on tight enough," Dad replied. "Baby muskrats know about water from the time they are born. Their mother will teach them all they have to know about swimming and diving to find food or shelter from danger."

We heard the twitter of a marsh wren. Dad steered the canoe close to a clump of cattails and pointed out its nest.

"It looks like a little African hut," Bob remarked.

I could see what he meant. Brown moss completely covered the top of the nest, leaving only a small hole for mother wren to leave or enter.

"The wind will rock her babies to sleep," I chuckled.

For some time we had heard sharp little bird twitters in the grass, but we had not seen the shy musician. Dad steered the canoe close to the bank. Suddenly a small, brown bird skittered from its hiding place, then pattered across the creek on lily pads.

"A snipe," Dad said.

"It didn't even get its feet wet," Bob marveled. "What would happen if it fell in?"

"Snipes can swim. They would just rather stay on top of the water than in it."

Our canoe grounded on a sandy bottom so we pushed off to deeper water.

"There used to be a beaver dam here," Dad pointed out. "High water has gradually washed it away.".

We caught a glimpse of a mink humping along a run in the bushes, and startled a mother grouse who had brought her young to the creek for a bedtime drink. Bob was first to see an early flying owl. I hoped that all the little critters we had seen would be safe from its sharp eyes and sharp talons.

Around the next bend was the biggest surprise of all: a large black animal stood almost submerged in the creek bed. Bob and I gasped as a huge antlered head rose out of the water, its mouth streaming with lily roots.

"A *moose!*" Bob said excitedly.

"Quiet!" Dad cautioned. "We'll see how close we can get."

"Careful, Dad." Bob sounded worried, but then he was closest to it.

With silent strokes, Dad urged the canoe closer while the moose continued to feed. Not until we were within two canoe lengths did it turn and lumber to the bank. It stood there, long ears high and questioning, as we glided by.

"Why isn't it afraid of us?" I whispered.

"I suspect it didn't recognize us as people when we are in the canoe," Dad explained. "Anyway, moose usually depend on their nose to warn them of danger. There isn't any wind tonight, so it wouldn't smell us. I once paddled as close as ten feet from a moose before it moved. Well, I think it's time we headed back to camp."

As we retraced out route, muskrats and beaver put on another show for our benefit. Duck wings whistled in the twilight. When we reached the entrance to the lake, a flock of geese came gliding in for a landing on a marshy shore.

"This has been an exciting evening," Bob exclaimed as we beached the canoe on the shore nearest to our tent. "And I thought it was just a dull old marsh!"

"Just a marsh, to be sure," Dad chuckled. "But it's never dull. To a lot of furred and feathered folk, it's the very best home. I'm glad we had a chance to visit them tonight."

"Me, too," I agreed. "I can't wait to do it again!"

Some Kind Of Mutt!

"HI! HI! HI!" I LEANED OVER Dick's neck and urged him on. Ahead of him, the band of horses swept towards the corral gate, manes and tails flying, hooves thundering on the meadow turf. One little pinto broke from the herd, bent on escape.

"No you don't!" I shouted, turning Dick. Foiled in its rebellion, the pinto joined the others.

I grinned, conscious of the fact that I had an audience. Uncle Pete and his friend, Larry Bartlett, were sitting on the corral fence. I could see that Mr. Bartlett had his movie camera ready to film the racing herd. Sure, it was only for a home movie, but it would be fun to show what a good rider I was.

Now I was close enough to see that the camera was in action. I sat up straight in the saddle and waved my hat. Wow! Would this be a good movie!

Then it happened—disaster. Shameful, humiliating disaster!

It was all because of Duke, that tawny, droop-eared dog. He had been crouched near the entrance to the corral and, as the horses thundered up, he dashed from his hiding place.

Rowf! Rowf! Rowf! Duke barked excitedly.

"Get back, Duke! Get out of there!" I shouted angrily. It was too late. Startled, the herd braked, then cut back. I tried desperately to flank them and would have, too, if Dick had not stepped into a hole. Already off balance, Dick stumbled, then lost his footing completely. I went flying over his head and ended up in a dusty heap. My head hit the ground and filled with a zillion stars.

Angry and humiliated, I recovered my hat, shook the dust off my clothes and recovered Dick.

"You miserable, flea-bitten, useless hound!" I yelled at Duke. "I could tan your hide and use it for a saddle blanket!"

Hardly the brightest of dogs, Duke could nevertheless

sense that he had done something wrong. His drooping ears sagged even further. He turned and scuttled under the fence to cower behind Bob.

"You're not hurt, are you?" Uncle Pete asked anxiously. "That was a nasty tumble."

"No, I'm not hurt," I grunted. "But just wait until I get my hands on that dog!"

Duke drew even farther back and peered between Bob's legs. He looked so worried that Uncle Pete laughed.

"That's quite a dog," Mr. Bartlett said. "He should be a lot of help to you when he's trained a little better. What kind is he? Collie?"

"I dunno," I said, rubbing the bump on my head. "He's just a dog, some kind of mutt."

"Well, he knows he did something wrong," Uncle Pete said. "And that's the first step in learning to do something right."

"That's the trouble," I muttered under my breath. "He can't do *anything* right!"

The horses had trotted out the open gate at the end of the corral and were gone. With Duke tagging along at my heels in disgrace, I set out again in pursuit of the herd. They had taken advantage of my fall to take a good head start. It could take hours to find them.

It was only last week, I reflected, that Duke had tangled with a porcupine and received a noseful of quills.

23

It took us an hour to get them all pulled out. Before the porcupine was the skunk. Duke had encountered it behind the house at night. He decided to give chase and had to sleep in the barn for a week.

"Crazy mutt! When are you going to get some sense?" I called back. Duke looked up and wagged his tail. He sensed that I wasn't angry any longer.

It was easy to follow the stray herd as long as they stayed on the dusty wagon road. I was drowsy from the sun's warmth and my head hurt—maybe that was why I didn't notice where they turned off into the woods. I retraced my steps and found their turning point, but it was hard to track them on the hard ground, and before long I lost the tracks altogether.

"If you were worth your keep, you'd track those horses for me," I scolded Duke. My head ached and I had trouble focusing on the trail. At that point I came to a spring and dismounted for a drink. I splashed water over my face, hoping to ease the pain in my head. Perhaps if I sat in the shade for a bit it would help.

I don't know how long I sat there, but suddenly I realized that the sun was shining in my face. I must have dozed off. I looked around for Dick but he was nowhere in sight.

"How careless can a person get!" I muttered angrily.

Some Kind Of Mutt!

Duke could see that he had done something wrong.
His drooping ears sagged even further.

"I should have tied him to a tree. I'll bet he headed for home."

I tried to get to my feet, but stopped, puzzled. My head throbbed worse than before and everything began spinning.

"I must have sat in the sun too long," I thought. "I'll dunk my head in the spring and rest in the shade awhile longer. That should make me feel better.

It didn't. I was still dizzy and nauseous. For a moment I couldn't recall where I was. Something was wrong, seriously wrong!

I held my head and tried to think. Somehow I had to find help. It was less than three miles back to the ranch, but it might as well have been ten because I couldn't walk. And Dick was gone.

Dick! I had a gleam of hope. Dick must surely have gone home. When he showed up without me my folks would know something was wrong. But how would they know where to look for me?

While I was trying to think, I felt a cool nose thrust against my cheek. Duke was still with me. I recalled reading a story where a faithful dog had gone for help when his master was injured. If only I could get Duke to take a message home!

Bob and I always carried a small pocket emergency kit. Among the items in my kit was a pencil stub and a folded slip of paper. Resting the paper on my knee, I drew a rough map. Bob would know this spring. Next to the map I scribbled, "Need help!"

"Come here, Duke," I called. The words stuck in my throat. With fingers that were all thumbs, I wrapped the note around Duke's collar and tied it with a piece of string.

"Go home, Duke!" I commanded. Duke merely looked at me curiously.

"Go home! Git!" I picked up a stick and flung it. Duke's response was to drop his tail between his legs and slink off to the edge of the clearing. It was obvious that he was not going to leave me alone.

My eyes filled with tears of frustration and fear. I scolded Duke until my voice grew hoarse, but it was no use. Duke crept up close to me and nuzzled me with his nose. That's all I remember.

When I opened my eyes, it was not the spring that I saw. I was lying in my own bed, with Mom and Dad looking down at me anxiously and Bob standing at the foot.

"Mom?"

"It's all right, Gary. You're safe now." There were tears of relief in her eyes.

"Wha...what happened? What's wrong with me?" I asked.

"It was that fall, Gary. You struck your head harder

27

than you realized. ~~You had a concussion.~~ It's a wonder you were able to go as far as you did."

I thought for a few moments, then I remembered. "I tried to send a message with Duke, but the stupid dog wouldn't go home! How did you find me?"

"It was Duke after all," Dad explained. "When Dick came home, we started out to look for you. From the tracks we could see in the dust, we were pretty sure you had gone up the valley. But we would have gone right by if it hadn't been for Duke. He heard us and barked as loud as he could. Believe it or not, he led us right to you."

"Well, good old Duke!" I burst out. "You know, I think I owe him an apology. He may be just a *mutt*, but to me he's the best dog a guy ever had!"

Flowers of the Forest

I WAS GIVING MOM A HAND with the weekly washing when Bob burst into the kitchen.

"Hey Gary, I've got a surprise for you!"

"A surprise! What kind of a surprise?"

"You will just have to wait and see! Come on, I'll take you there. It's only a couple of miles."

"Okay, just wait until I finish this tub." Fortunately it was the last load.

We had a lot of surprises on our wilderness ranch. Sometimes Dad or Mom pointed them out to us,

sometimes we discovered them on our own. It wasn't often that one of us found something surprising without the other knowing; we were almost always together.

I needed no urging to saddle Dick and follow Bob on his horse Tony down the pasture trail. It was spring and the air was filled with the fragrance of pollinating pine trees. The woods echoed with the mating calls of dozens of birds. It was great to be alive!

We let ourselves through the gate at the end of the pasture and followed a game trail through thick lodgepole pine. I knew that this trail led to a spring cradled in a spruce swamp. It was a watering place both for wildlife and for our own cattle and horses.

"We have to walk from here," Bob announced. "It's too soft for the horses. Here, tie up to this tree."

I was growing more curious by the minute. It was clear to me that the surprise was not going to be a wild animal; Bob was making no attempt to be quiet. Could it be a hawk nest? What had Bob discovered in this isolated swamp?

Bob led the way, moving carefully to avoid sinking into the mud. Finally he pushed through a clump of bushes and came to a stop. "There!"

"Wow!" I gasped. I was completely stunned. For a

dozen metres in front of me I saw a bright yellow carpet of flowers clustered on long stalks, swaying gracefully in the breeze. It was like a burst of sunshine filling the glade!

"What are they?" I stammered. I had never seen flowers like these before.

"Snapdragons," Bob replied, pleased by my reaction. "I found these when I was looking for the horses this morning. Dad told me what they are. There must not be a lot of them growing in this area—these are the first I've seen. Let's take a bouquet to Mom."

We picked a few of the flowers, being careful not to pull up the roots. Each root would produce a new plant to bloom next year.

With our northern winter lasting almost six months, we were grateful for the coming of spring and all the changing colours that came with it.

When the retreating snow left patches of new growth, Mom would send Bob and me to sunny slopes where the dandelions were the first to produce shoots. Hungry for greens, we brought in bowls of tender green leaves which Mom made into salads, or steamed for a delicious vegetable treat.

One day we would awaken to find our green slopes, from one end to the other, had become a golden carpet of dandelion blooms. As quickly as they came, they were gone, leaving in their place a puffy shawl of seed stalks. The first stiff wind carried the seeds away to multiply next year's gift of gold.

Each part of our new world had its own gift of colour. Even the dry fir ridges did not disappoint us. Bob and I were riding for stray cattle one day when suddenly Bob pulled Tony to a stop.

"Gary, just look at *that*!"

"Oh, they're beautiful!" was all I could say to describe the riot of colour before us. Scattered beneath the trees were thousands of pink and lavender flowers. When we dismounted for a closer look, we found that each bloom was shaped like a tiny slipper.

"Fairy slippers!" I suggested in awe.

I was not far wrong. When we looked them up in Mom's flower book, we learned that they were called *ladyslippers* and were a member of the orchid family. Their delicate blooms delighted us for a week before they, like the dandelions, were gone until another year.

One of my chores each morning was to bring in the milk cows from pasture. Sometimes I moved waist deep through wild rose bushes covered with fragrant blooms. For a while I picked bouquets of pink buds to take home to Mom. Each time I was disappointed.

Before I could get them to her they opened wide and all their petals fell off. Their flowers were for woodland display only.

In our first home in California, we found beautiful displays of wild lilies. That first spring, Bob and I wondered if we would find northern varieties.

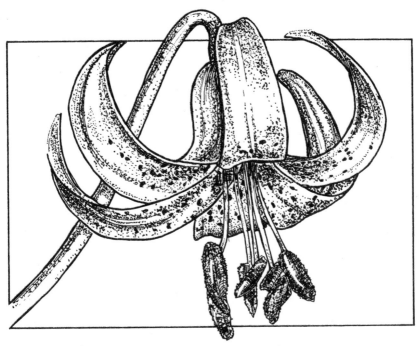

...he pointed out yellow, pumpkin-shaped blooms with tiny black freckles on each petal.

"Dad," I asked one day. "How come there aren't any lilies around here?"

Dad seemed to know more than me. Perhaps he had been talking to neighbours. "Just be patient, Gary, and keep your eyes open," he replied.

One day Dad came into the house just as Bob and I were finishing our school work for the day.

"Come with me, boys, I've got something to show you."

Filled with curiosity, we followed Dad through the garden and into the calf pasture. In a grove of poplar trees he pointed out yellow, pumpkin-shaped blooms with tiny black freckles on each petal.

"What did I tell you?" Dad grinned. "See, lilies—*tiger lilies*, to be correct."

"Wow! I can see why they are called tiger lilies," I marveled. "These are beautiful!"

It must have been the right year for tiger lilies. Before long we found them everywhere, sometimes a single bloom on a long, slender stalk, sometimes whole clusters.

A few weeks later we found other lilies. Bob and I rode to a lake at the far end of our range to troll for trout from a canoe. These lilies were an unexpected bonus.

"Just look at those blooms!" Bob exclaimed.

"There are a zillion of them!" I was impressed. I had never seen water lilies in bloom before.

The lilies grew in a broad border all around the lake shore. Their leaves were fifteen to twenty centimetres across and floated on the surface of the water. The blooms were cup-shaped and about eight centimetres in diameter. In some of the blooms, little frogs had found a fragrant place to laze in the sun.

Our next floral surprise was found in a grove of lodgepole pine. We had been studying about South America's rainforests where vines climbed on trunks of trees high enough to be lost in the canopy of the forest. To find something similar in our northern world was exciting. Our vines spiraled as much as six metres up the tree trunks, and produced great numbers of white, trumpet-shaped flowers. We raced home to find out what they were called.

"*Clematis*, wild clematis." Mom had the flower book open to the section on climbers. "They freeze in the winter, but grow from the roots every summer, sometimes as much as ten metres high."

"Hey Mom," I grinned. "Now that we have rainforest vines, do you think we'll discover monkeys next?"

No, we never found monkeys in our wilderness, but

we did find something that appreciated the flowers—ruby-throated hummingbirds that buzzed from flower to flower, sipping nectar. Dad amazed us when he said that hummingbirds wintered as far away as Central America.

"If they could talk, they could tell us all about rainforests," Bob suggested.

I suppose nature could function if everything were black and white, but how much more exciting it is when flowers give us all the colours of the rainbow to brighten our wilderness world.

Learning to Live

"HEY! WATCH OUT!"

An involuntary cry of warning escaped my lips as I jumped over a fallen fir tree. What on earth was happening?

"What is it?" Bob shouted from behind.

It took me some seconds to sort out what was happening on the ground in front of me. It was then that I realized I had almost dropped on top of a family picnic—or maybe it was a classroom. I saw a mother ruffled grouse with perhaps a dozen downy chicks!

Moments after I landed, mother

grouse seemed to go into hysterics. She flopped on her side uttering frantic cries as though badly injured. When I tried to get closer, she flopped away, dragging one wing. She looked helpless, but I could not put a hand on her. Bob moved in from another direction but he, too, had no luck. We must have followed her a hundred feet away when she took off, flying high into a tree.

"I wonder what that was all about?" Bob puzzled.

"I don't know, but I think she was trying to fool us or something," I replied, as puzzled as Bob.

"Do you suppose she was leading us away from her babies?"

"Now that you mention it, I wouldn't be surprised. Let's go back and see if we can find some of the chicks."

We returned to the place where we had first seen the family and searched as carefully as we could. There was not a chick to be seen, not a sound to be heard. They had completely disappeared!

"I have an idea. Let's sit down on the log and see what happens," I suggested. "Don't make a sound or a movement."

Perhaps ten minutes went by while nothing happened. We were ready to give up when we heard the mother grouse fly to the ground. Minutes later we saw her approaching, pausing every few steps to look and listen. Finally, satisfied that all was well, she gave a series of low clucking calls.

I blinked my eyes in surprise. From the very ground we had searched so closely, the baby grouse appeared. A leaf moved, and there was a downy chick; two more came from behind a fallen branch, another from a patch of moss, and so on until all clustered around their mother. It confirmed what we had suspected; while she created a disturbance around our feet the babies had followed her directions and hid. Not only that, they remained hidden until she called them back to her.

"I can hardly believe what my eyes tell me is true!" Bob exclaimed. "I wonder how she trained her chicks to do that?"

I shook my head. "There must be some way that they communicate to each other. It's beyond me!"

Isolated as Bob and I were on our ranch, we had opportunity to spend time in the wilderness around us observing wildlife in their own territory. We learned many things, but perhaps most interesting of all was the way birds and animals train their young in ways of survival.

Of course, Bob and I were also taught ways to survive, but not when we were babies a few weeks or months old.

In the spring we looked forward to eating small, cone-shaped mushrooms that grew in willow swamps or poplar groves. Finding them was one of the tasks Bob and I learned to do. One day I spotted some fine mushrooms and gathered them into my pail. Often where one is found, others grow nearby. I pressed more branches out of the way and cried out in surprise. Something brown and furry lay within inches of my hand!

"Bob! Come and see what I've found!"

"Huh? What is it, a bird's nest?" Bob came and looked over my shoulder.

Moving carefully, I spread the branches apart. Before our eyes was a tiny deer fawn with a tawny, spotted coat. It crouched flat against the ground, head tucked down between sharp little hooves, and long ears laid flat against its neck. Although its eyes were wide open, it did not so much as flick an eyelash.

"I wonder where its mother is?" I said, awed by such a surprising find.

We stood up and looked in every direction, but there was no sign of any other deer.

Dad had told us about how deer and moose hide their young when they go off to feed or there is danger about. Because the very young have no body scent, predators such as coyotes and wolves are unlikely to find them. Somehow the mothers train their young to follow directions and lie perfectly still. Dad told us, too, that we should not touch one of these woodland babies lest our scent should cause the mother to abandon her young.

"Lets walk off downwind and wait awhile," Bob

suggested. "Perhaps the doe will return."

We walked away for a hundred metres or so, then circled back to a knoll from which we could see the thicket where the fawn was hidden. For half an hour we remained still and silent. Finally our patience was rewarded. The doe picked her way softly through the woods, stopping frequently to look and listen. When she reached the fawn, it jumped to its feet, nuzzled its mother happily, then followed close at her heels as she led it away into the forest.

It crouched flat against the ground, head tucked down between sharp little hooves, and long ears laid flat against its neck.

Bob and I were excited at this discovery. We had found another way in which our woodland neighbours learn how to stay alive.

During that summer we discovered other examples of woodland survival classes. Much of this was concerned with finding food. The mother porcupine teaches her prickly young where sweet clover patches are to be found, and which trees have tender bark that can be eaten at any time of the year.

The squirrel family seems to be playing an endless game of tag as its members leap from tree to tree. In reality, the parents are teaching their young to search out cones that have seeds and nuts inside. Even the young are expected to carry these cones to the underground storehouses that will hold food for the cold winter months to come.

Learning obedience without hesitation is one of the most important lessons the young must learn, especially if they are the kind that might provide supper for a predator.

One evening Bob and I rode our horses several miles to see a beaver dam, discovered by our Dad a few days earlier. We stopped well away from the dam and tied our horses to a tree.

"We'll have to sneak up on the dam without making a sound," Bob cautioned. "Dad says the older beavers always have someone on watch."

"Do you think we'll see them cutting down trees?" I had often seen the chiseled stumps left by beaver, but never saw a tree actually being felled.

"Shhh...stay quiet or we won't see anything at all!"

We were fortunate in that the scent-carrying breeze was blowing away from the dam. The beavers would not detect us in that manner.

Finally we reached the edge of the small canyon in which the beavers had built their dam.

"Let's crawl up behind those bushes." Bob led the way, moving carefully to avoid the snap of a twig.

We reached our observation point, apparently without causing any alarm. Our diligence in stalking was rewarded. We could see that several beavers were swimming about the pond.

"See those two over there?" I whispered. "They're much smaller than the others."

"Probably this year's kits," Bob whispered back. "Maybe the parents are teaching the young ones how to look after the dam."

I nodded, but I couldn't see that any work was being done. "Maybe it's recess time."

The owl must have been perched on a tree near the water. Suddenly it swept past our viewpoint and plunged on silent wings towards one of the kits. We both gasped in surprise and dismay. Would the young beaver provide supper for the owl?

At that moment there was a loud report as father beaver's tail slammed down on the surface of the pond. Instantly the young beaver dove. So close was the escape, the owl actually struck the water. Had the kit hesitated to obey so much as a moment, it would have been carried away by the twilight predator.

"Wow!" I let my breath rush out in a loud sigh of relief. "That was close!"

"You bet it was!" Bob agreed. "I thought that little guy was a goner!"

We found other ways in which woodland young were taught to survive, the hunted from the hunters, but perhaps none in so graphic a manner as that of the beaver family.

From our neighbours of feather and fur, Bob and I discovered something of value for ourselves: good habits, learned while we are young, can be helpful to us the rest of our lives!

Operation Birdlift

"BOB, WHAT ARE THOSE BIRDS doing?" I asked, watching a swirling flock of birds flutter along the creek bank.

"I don't know, Gary. It looks to me like they're picking up something. Let's get a closer look."

This was our first year on an isolated Cariboo cattle ranch, and there was much to learn about our neighbours of fur and feather. Over the winter months we had great fun skiing and tobogganing, and learning about the survival skills of birds and animals. Now it was spring.

I followed my brother along the edge of the stream, moving carefully so we would not frighten the birds.

"You know what? I think they're picking up mud!" Bob exclaimed.

The birds were coming and going in a steady stream, swooping out of the sky to the ground, then flying away again. I tried to focus on a single bird to find out what it was doing.

"Look, Bob, they're flying into the loft of the barn! Do you suppose they are building nests?"

"Let's go see!" Bob led the way.

The barn was built of logs cut from the surrounding forest. The lower level held stalls to shelter the horses through the winter months, while the loft, below a steeply pitched roof, was for hay storage. Bob and I spent many happy hours in the loft, jumping and tumbling in the hay.

"Careful of that ladder," Bob warned. Older than me, he felt responsible for my safety.

"They *are* building nests!" I cried out. "See, Bob, lots and lots of nests!"

Dozens of busy builders were at work, chirping and flitting in and out of the loft. The shingles of the roof were nailed onto pole rafters. In the vee where shingles met poles, the birds were building dome-shaped nests out of the mud they carried from the creek.

"How do they make them stay there?" Bob wondered. The nests were hung upside down, defying gravity.

"Dad is coming," I said from my perch by the window. "He knows all about birds; let's ask him."

Drawn by our calls, Dad joined us in the loft.

"See what those birds are doing, Dad?" I pointed to the rafters. "What kind of birds are they?"

"They're *swallows*, son—barn swallows. They spent the winter in the south and now they've come back to nest. That's good news."

"What do you mean, Dad? Why is it good news?"

"Because each swallow eats hundreds of mosquitoes every day. You don't know much about mosquitoes yet, but in a few weeks you will know why it's good news to have them thinned out."

"I know—they bite!" Bob chuckled. "We had lots of them at Camp last summer."

"I'll say they bite! But our friends the swallows will help keep them down," Dad replied.

"Dad, I know they're building nests, but Bob and I can't understand how they hang them up there. Why don't they fall down?"

"Because they have a special way of doing it. They secrete a sticky substance from their saliva and mix it with the mud they carry in their beaks. It helps them cement the mud to the rafters, and mud to mud."

"Hey, that's clever!" Bob said. "Is there a reason why they build their nests in the barn instead of in trees like other birds do?"

"Well, think about it, Bob. The roof shelters them from wind and rain and things that might harm their young. Can you imagine a cat getting up there?"

Bob grinned. "It would have to be equipped with suction feet."

In the days ahead, we came often to watch the swallows, whenever our chores took us near the barn. In a surprisingly short time the nests were finished, each one ending with a hole just large enough for the parent birds to enter.

"They must like neighbours," I remarked. Each nest was stuck to the next one and each rafter held ten or fifteen nests. The loft rang with the merry chatter of the swallows. One day we noticed that the chatter had stopped.

"The mother birds have laid their eggs and are sitting on them until they hatch," Dad explained.

When several weeks had passed, Bob and I heard a chorus of cheeps from the loft. The baby birds were hatching!

Now the parent birds were on the move again, swooping out of the barn to weave circles in the sky, darting back to bring food to their babies. Each time they

Each time they returned there was frantic cheeping as the young fought to be fed first.

returned there was frantic cheeping as the young fought to be fed first.

"I know what's happening," Bob said excitedly. "They're catching mosquitoes in the air."

One day dark clouds rolled out of the west. Bob and I were picking mushrooms when the flash of lightning and the boom of thunder sent us scurrying for home. By the time we reached the pasture gate big drops of rain began to fall.

"Quick, into the barn!" Bob panted. "We'll wait there until the storm goes by."

We were just in time. Great gusts of wind made the barn shudder, while thunder crashed until we held our hands over our ears. The rain came down in sheets, turning the barnyard into sticky mud. Little trickles became streams as runoff water cut paths to the creek, turning it into chocolate milk.

Finally the thunder grew fainter, the rain slackened and then stopped. Black clouds moved away to the east and the sun came out, making the ground steam. We could safely leave our shelter.

"Listen!" I cocked my head to one side. "Why are those swallows so excited?"

Above our heads the air was filled with cries of distress. The parent birds were flying in aimless circles, screeching excitedly. Then we heard a new sound—frantic cheeping in the hay loft.

"Come on, let's see what happened," Bob shouted. He scrambled up the ladder to the loft. I was close behind.

In the loft we found a tragic scene. The force of the wind had driven rainwater under the shingles where it had seeped into many of the nests. Several dozen had given way and fallen to the hay below. In the crumbled wreckage were baby swallows, half-grown but unable to fly. Their cries of fear filled the loft and were echoed by the frantic parents.

"Oh, Bob, the poor little birds! What can we do to help?" I cradled several little ones in my hands. Feeling the warmth of my skin, they cuddled together and stopped their crying.

"We can't leave them here, something will eat them for sure," Bob said. His eyes swept upward to the remaining nests and the frantic parent birds who still wheeled and cried in dismay. "Hey—I have an idea!"

"We'll take them to the house?" I guessed. I wasn't sure what Mom would say about that!

"No, that wouldn't be any good. We couldn't look after them all. But see, Gary, a lot of those nests are close to the back wall of the barn. I'm sure I could reach them with a ladder."

"You mean we could put the babies in other nests?" I felt doubtful about that.

51

"Sure. That way they would be safe. You gather them together in one place; I'll get the long ladder."

It worked! Bob climbed the ladder until he was close to the nests. With baby birds cradled in pockets of my jacket, I climbed up behind Bob and passed the chicks to him. Bob popped two into each nest he could reach.

When all of the nests had their share, there were still a dozen or more chicks left over. Bob climbed higher until he could reach the hayfork trolley that ran the length of the roof. All the remaining birds were given safe perches along this retreat, then we climbed down to watch what would happen.

"Do you think it will work?" I asked.

"We'll have to wait and see," Bob replied.

Soon the frantic cries quieted. The parent birds seemed to sense that the crisis was over. We were delighted to see that all the babies were being fed.

"You know what, Bob? We just happened to be here at the right time. Maybe it wasn't just an accident; maybe we were meant to be here! What do you think?"

Bob chuckled. "You may be right. Let's just say we were sent on a secret mission. Hey, I know! We'll call it *Operation Birdlift!*"

A Snap In The Dark

CHIK, CHIK, CHIK...RRRR!

Around the gnarled trunk of a spruce tree came a red squirrel, fussing and scolding and demanding to know what was going on.

"Scat!" Bob hissed and snapped his fingers impatiently.

Up went the squirrel's bushy tail while its strident complaint grew in volume. *Chik...rrr, chik-chik-chik...rrr!*

Any wild ears within hearing range would get the message: "Take care, something is wrong here!"

I wadded up a clutch of moss and lobbed it at the self-appointed sentry. My aim was good; the missile dropped squarely on its bobbing head. Yipping in alarm, the squirrel scurried to safer territory near the top of the tree. There it continued to scold until an early flying owl forced it to prudent silence.

The sun slipped down behind the hills and already shadows were moving across the muskeg. Somewhere a pine beetle chirped. Bob eased himself to a sitting position while his eyes searched the surrounding area for signs of life.

"See anything?" I whispered.

"Not a thing." Bob sighed. "I think we picked the right place, but maybe it's the wrong night."

It was Larry Bartlett who started it. He owned a photography shop in California and accompanied our aunt and uncle when they visited our ranch. Bob and I had taken him to some of the scenic spots of our area so he could record them on film. After Larry had returned to California, he sent us a camera, complete with flash. We decided to build an album of wildlife photos. We already had pictures of a deer and of beaver at work; now we wanted a picture of a moose.

"You will have a hard time getting that close to a moose," Dad said, when he heard about our project.

"We have a plan," Bob replied. "Just give us time."

Our plan was to find a frequently used moose trail and set up our camera and flash in such a way that we could set it off while hiding. We thought we had found the perfect spot. Near a swamp two miles from home we found a game trail that followed a rail fence into a small meadow. Close by was a haystack where we could hide in comfort and see anything that approached. We tied the camera to the fence at the right height and attached a string to the shutter. Working together, we unrolled the string until it reached the top of the haystack. If a moose came down the trail we might just get the close-up picture we coveted. That was all we needed—a cooperative moose!

"If it gets much darker it will be hard to tell when a moose is in the right position," I worried.

"I've got a marker," Bob explained. "When a moose gets to the corner of the fence, he will be in the right place. I'll be able to see the fence for quite awhile yet."

I wet my finger and held it up, testing the wind. What breeze there was came from the direction of the camera. It wouldn't betray our presence to a moose.

"Look over there!" I hissed and pointed. "I'm sure something moved!"

"Just a shadow..." Bob began, then stopped short. Something *did* move.

We both strained to see what was causing the willows to sway, then chuckled. A gangling coyote pup dashed

~~from the shadows and pounced for something, a mouse~~
we guessed.

For several minutes we watched the coyote's leaps and dashes as he pursued the mouse. Obviously inexperienced in the art of hunting for his supper, the pup finally gave up and trotted away.

CRACK!

Somewhere a twig snapped. We froze. Absorbed in watching the coyote's antics, we had neglected to watch the trail.

CLICK, CLATTER, THUMP!

Cautiously we turned our heads to peer up the trail. It was now so dark at the edge of the woods we had difficulty telling one shadow from another. But there was no doubt about the message our ears picked up: some large animal was approaching.

"There it is!" I whispered tensely.

"Shhhh," Bob cautioned.

No doubt about it now. We could make out the dim outline of a large moose moving cautiously along the game trail. Suddenly it stopped and held its head high, testing the wind for danger. We waited in suspense, scarcely daring to breathe. Would the moose detect our presence and shy away?

Bob let out his breath in a sigh of relief as the moose continued its way down the trail. It was almost time to

There was a moose, all of a moose, but not what we expected.

trip the camera.

"The string!" Bob hissed. "I dropped the string." He groped frantically around him in the hay.

"Hurry!" I whispered back. "It's almost there! Now, Bob, pull the string!"

"I've found it!" Bob gasped. He gave the elusive string a sharp tug. The darkness exploded into sudden light as the flash went off. In the instant before shadows took over again, we saw a swift movement of legs and a black rump at the edge of the light. With a loud snort, the moose swung away in panic.

"Too late!" Bob burst out in savage frustration. "It had already gone past the camera! How could I have been so stupid as to drop that string?"

"We can try again tomorrow night," I suggested hopefully.

"Sure we can—but we'll never get another chance like that!" Bob mourned.

We climbed off the stack and made our way along the meadow to the thicket where we had tied our horses. We found to our dismay that the horses were gone, probably spooked by the fleeing moose. We would find them at the barn gate, waiting to be unsaddled. Too disappointed to talk, we stumbled along the darkened trail for home.

Next morning we awakened to overcast skies. By noon the rain was falling soddenly, the way it did when we

were in for days of storm.

A few days later, Dad announced that he was going to ride to the General Store. We decided to send our film to be developed. We had taken a picture of a porcupine; perhaps that would turn out right.

It was two weeks later when the snaps were returned in the mail. Bob tore open the packet and shook the photos out on the table so we could see what we had. Suddenly he gasped.

"Gary, just look at this!"

"What is it, the back end of a moose?"

It was my turn to gasp. There was a moose, all of a moose, but not what we expected. It was a moose calf, frozen in surprise by the light of the flash!

"It must have been following right behind its mother," Bob shouted with delight. "We were so busy thinking about the big moose we didn't even see the calf!"

"So, we got a picture of a moose after all," I exclaimed. "Now, want to try for a bear?"

Midnight Ride

BOB AND I HAD JUST FINISHED filling the wood boxes when Dad arrived home from the Post Office. We walked with him to the barn to put Gerry in his stall.

"I learned some good news today," Dad said.

"What kind of good news?" Bob and I were instantly alert. Most of the time "good news" waited until spring, so isolated were the ranchers.

"You know that heifer we were missing at roundup? Well, I met Alexander from Halfway Ranch in the General Store. He said the heifer is on his feedlot. He hadn't noticed her at first because her long winter hair hid the brand."

"Say, that is good news," Bob exclaimed. We were sure she must have been killed by a wolf or a bear when she didn't show up with the others. It wasn't unusual for us to lose one or more head of cattle each year to rangeland marauders. Sometimes they had two feet instead of four!

"Our next problem is how to get her back to where she belongs," Dad went on. "Even if we could afford a truck to go in there for her, the snow is too deep for it to come up our road."

"We could leave her there until spring and pay Alexander to feed her," I suggested.

"I thought about that," Dad replied. "But she would get used to running with his cattle. Next summer we'd have trouble keeping her on our range."

Well, I guess that means Bob and I had better ride over there and get her," I concluded. "It's only about ten miles across country."

"The snow will be deep on the other end," Dad said doubtfully. "It would be a long, cold ride."

"Oh, we don't mind," Bob said. "We can follow the sleigh road to our hay meadow for the first four miles and that will be easy going. If we get an early start we can get back to good road before dark."

"All right. If you are willing to go, I'll leave it up to

you. You'd better start tomorrow morning, though. The way that wind is blowing we could have a change to colder weather."

Soon after daylight the next day, I saddled Dick and Bob saddled Tony, then we headed out at a brisk trot. There would be a lot of trail to break on the other end of the journey so we wanted to make good time on the hard-packed sleigh road. We weren't worried about finding the way, but it would be a lonely ride, especially after dark.

When we reached the lakes we saw that the wind had blown most of the snow from the ice.

"Hey, I have an idea," Bob said. "Let's follow the ice up to the other end. That will give us another two miles of easy traveling."

"Do you think it's safe?" I wondered.

"Safe as a paved highway," Bob assured me. "That ice must be at least a foot thick."

"All right, let's do it."

Dick and Tony were not happy about our change of route. They shied whenever the lake groaned or the ice cracked, and they didn't like the sound of their hooves on the hard surface. We knew that such noises were common on the lake whenever there was a change in temperature.

We went on at a swift trot. It wasn't just the long trip that we were anxious about. Behind us in the west a long gray blanket of cloud moved up to cover the blue of the winter sky. A freshening wind warned us that we were in for another storm.

Half way up the lakes we saw three moving black dots, perhaps half a mile away. Our horses saw them at the same time and snorted loudly.

"Do you see that?" Bob said excitedly. "Those are wolves, you can bet on that!"

"Yeah, I see them. Do you think it's safe to go on?"

We had seen what wolves could do to one of our cattle, and sometimes a horse. Their standard hunting practice was to leap onto the back of an animal, bite through its spine and bring it down. The pack could then begin to feed whether or not the animal was dead. Wolves were no friends of ranchers.

"They won't bother us, or our horses while we are riding them," Bob assured me. "It's a good thing, though, that the heifer is on Alexander's feedlot, not out on the range."

The wolves trotted off the lake and disappeared in the woods. I couldn't help but notice that if they continued in that direction, they would cut the trail we would be riding.

Before we reached the end of the lake we heard the wolves howling in the manner they do when they are running a quarry. No doubt they had found a moose.

Still, a full-grown moose could fight off a wolf attack. They would likely opt for an old animal or last spring's calf.

When it was our turn to leave the lakes, we found the snow was much deeper than we expected. We had been climbing steadily since leaving our home ranch, and snow was always deeper at higher altitudes. Here it was up to our stirrups, a good metre deep. Dick and Tony didn't like it, but they had sturdy legs and were grain fed. We knew they could handle it. Still, we took turns breaking trail.

It was past noon when we rode in to the feedlot at Halfway Ranch. The sky was completely clouded over and a few snowflakes drifted down.

"Come on in and warm yourselves," the tall young rancher invited as we pulled up in front of his cabin. We saw little of our neighbours during winter, and a warm welcome was assured whenever we met.

"Thanks," Bob replied. "We really should be heading back, but our horses need a rest, and so do we. We'll accept your invitation."

Mrs. Alexander served us a hot lunch while we exchanged news of the district. It was hard to tear ourselves away, but we knew there were less than four hours of daylight left. It would be good to reach the lakes again before dark.

It was not difficult to locate our heifer, as we knew just what she looked like. Getting her away from the feedlot was another matter. It took all three of us riding hard to cut her out of the herd and get her moving down our back trail.

"I don't envy you that ride," Alexander said as he pulled up to turn home. "Better keep her moving right along. Wind feels as though we're in for some real weather!"

"I think you're right," I shot back. "We'll hustle along."

"And thank you for taking care of our heifer," Bob called over his shoulder.

"That's what neighbours are for," Alexander called back. With a wave of his hand he was gone, quickly swallowed up by the snow.

Right from the start the heifer made it plain that she didn't want to leave her friends. We couldn't blame her. The snow was well up on her sides; if it hadn't been for our earlier trail-breaking, she would have been unable to go.

The wind steadily increased in force and, because we were now heading into it, we were soon covered with snow. What was worse, the trail was rapidly drifting in. This was serious. For the first time I was beginning to wonder if we had made a mistake in attempting the drive.

Darkness—earlier than usual because of the blanket

of clouds—closed in before we had covered half the distance to the lakes. We seemed to be riding into a black tunnel under the trees, hardly able to make out the brown blur of the heifer. More and more frequently, the heifer plunged off the trail and would move again only after one or the other of us bumped her with our horses. We crossed an open swamp and were dismayed to find our trail filled in with drifting snow. Now, one of us had to go ahead and break trail while the other urged the heifer to follow.

One of us had to go ahead and break trail while the other urged the heifer to follow.

Bob called a halt and eased his horse up to mine. "You know, if this gets any worse, we're not going to make it tonight," he said. "We might have to go back to the Halfway Ranch."

"Oh, no," I groaned. "It's nearly as far back there as it is to the lake. If we can even reach our sleigh road, we shouldn't have any trouble."

Bob thought a moment. "Yeah, I guess you're right. One thing is sure, we can't leave the heifer here—the wolves would get her before morning!"

Even as we paused in the snow, we heard the distant howl of a wolf, more frightening still because of the blackness of the night and the swirling snow.

"So be it," I shot back. "Let's get going! I'll break trail for awhile."

After what seemed like endless hours, the trees opened ahead of us. We both sighed with relief when we saw the open ice. I don't believe the heifer could have bucked through the snow much longer.

Now that some of the anxiety of the drive was past, I began to feel the effects of stabbing snow and long hours in the saddle. I was hungry, too, and thought longingly of the crackling fire in our old ranch house, of a hot meal waiting on the back of the stove, and of the light in the window that Mom never failed to place when one of us was out in the dark.

We reached the meadow and moved on down the sleigh road, making better time now that we didn't have to break trail. To cheer our weary way, we began to sing, making echoes in the black of the night. That should scare the wolves away!

Too tired to sing any more, we lapsed into silence and rode side by side, slowing our horses to match the tired heifer's pace. I couldn't stop yawning.

Suddenly I jerked straight, startled and confused. I had fallen asleep in the saddle. And so had Bob!

"Hey Bob, come alive—we've both been asleep!"

"Huh? Oh, yeah, I guess you're right. Say, where's the heifer?"

"Oh no—we've lost her!" I could hardly believe that she was no longer in front of us.

Wearily, we turned around. A quarter mile back up the sleigh road we found our heifer. She had turned off the track and was huddled under a tree, eating from a pile of hay that had slid from one of Dad's hayloads.

"Come on, you wretched beast!" Bob shouted. "You want to get eaten by wolves?"

It was past midnight when we saw the glimmer of a light through the trees, signaling that our long journey was over. We had been in the saddle more than fifteen hours, and were numb with cold and fatigue. We turned the heifer into the feedlot with the other cattle.

"I'll bet she isn't even thankful we brought her home," Bob grumbled.

"No danger of her going back to the Halfway Ranch, not in this snow," I replied. "Come on, we've done our job; now it's time for Mom's hot stew—and bed. No more midnight rides for me!"

A Brother's Courage

"WOW! JUST LOOK AT THAT ice!" Bob shouted, pointing at the lake ahead of us. "Smooth as glass and a mile long!"

Dad had ridden by Eagle Lake two miles from our ranch home on the previous day and noted how smooth the ice was. He asked if we would like to try skating. Mom gave us a half-day off from our studies so we could take advantage of the ice before snow fell again. We were eager to go.

Next morning it was -16°C, but that didn't bother us; we were used to much colder temperatures than that. What mattered was that no snow had fallen overnight. The three miles to Eagle Lake was no problem either. We were looking for some real fun on the ice.

We tied our horses to a tree and raced to see who could get his skates on first. Bob won but I wasn't far behind him.

"Hey, this is great!" I shouted as I swooped along the shore. "Pass me the puck!" We had received hockey sticks for Christmas, and now put them to good use. Even though we were too isolated to play on a hockey team, we had lots of fun passing the puck between us.

"Better not go out too far," Bob warned. "There are springs in this lake. Remember when the moose went through the ice?"

I remembered. The springs were treacherous things that caused ice to freeze only enough to hide the danger beneath. The moose that plunged through the ice couldn't struggle out again. Wolves and coyotes had eaten all that was left above the surface.

I passed the puck towards the shoreline where Bob caught it deftly on the tip of his stick. He set it skittering back across the ice ahead of me. Knowing I wouldn't be able to reach the puck I swerved hard, intent only on stopping the puck.

"Watch out!" Bob shouted. He could see what I didn't—a change in the surface of the ice ahead of me. At the same time there was a threatening crack beneath my skates as I turned in panic towards the shore.

"KEE...RACK!" Like a broken window, the ice split in all directions and began to sink beneath my flailing skates. Even in my terror, I had sense enough to throw myself flat on the ice, arms and legs flung wide. It was too late! The ice gave way beneath me and in another moment I felt a shock of fear as icy water swallowed my thrashing body to the shoulders. Torn from my grip, my hockey stick clattered away out of reach.

"Bob!" I screamed. "Help me, I'm sinking!" Frantically I tried to climb out, but the ice only broke under my hands. I was terrified that I would slip under the ice itself.

"Don't panic!" Bob stopped a safe distance away and surveyed the situation. "Lie flat, Gary. Keep your arms on the ice!"

This I was trying to do, but my heavy, wet clothes were leaden, pulling me down. I recalled the moose's fate.

"I c...c...can't hold on!" I cried. "I'm going to d...d...drown!" I trembled with cold and fear.

Bob skated towards me—agonizingly slow it seemed to me. Still, I knew he had to be careful or he would end up in the lake, too. Finally Bob lay flat on the ice, inching himself along with the tip of his skates. On he came: five feet, ten feet—the ice cracked! He stopped.

Teeth chattering like castanets, I watched in

frightened fascination as water moved across the ice to meet him.

"Stretch your arm out as far as you can reach." Bob spoke quietly, trying to calm my panic. I did as he ordered. He moved his hockey stick out towards me, straining; it wouldn't reach. I could see him frown as he looked at the ice, testing it with his eyes. Then he began to inch forward. Again the ice cracked ominously.

"C...c...careful," I stammered.

The hockey stick closed the distance between us: six inches, two. My straining fingers touched the wood, then closed around it. Still moving slowly, Bob crept backwards, pulling on the stick. The ice sank in front of me and water welled up, but this was a help for it buoyed me up. The moments seemed like hours. Now I felt the ice hold beneath me; then Bob was helping me to my feet. Safe!

"Let's head for home!" I shouted.

"No!" Bob declared firmly. "You would freeze before we got there!" He was right, of course. Already my pants were stiff, and water dripping off my shoulders froze in tiny icicles down the front of my coat. I had never been so cold in my life!

"We've got to get a fire going." Bob raced on ahead. "Come and help me get wood, don't stand still."

It was good advice. Soon we had a stack of dry limbs

piled high in the shelter of an overhanging willow clump. Bob reached in his pocket for matches, frowned, then searched another pocket. Nothing.

"Don't you have matches?" I asked anxiously. I searched through my own pockets and found a pack. No use, they were soaking wet.

"I c...c...can't hold on!" I cried. "I'm going to d...d...drown!"
I trembled with cold and fear.

"I was sure I took matches before we left home; how could I have been so forgetful?" Again Bob searched his pockets. "Ah…" He sighed with relief as he pulled a match from his shirt pocket. It was broken in half but the head was intact. Carefully he drew together tufts of dry grass, then struck the match on a stone. Trembling, I watched the tiny flame catch in the grass, flare up to eat into the dry twigs, then spread into a cheery blaze.

I stood so close to the fire my clothes began to smoke. Gradually the heat penetrated the frosted garments. I could feel the numbness receding as life-giving heat drove the killing cold from my body.

Sometime later, when my clothes had dried enough to hold the warmth, we rode home, Bob leading the way along the woodland trail.

I was shaken by my narrow escape, but grateful for my rescue. This wasn't the first time Bob had saved me. Sometimes little brothers have to take second place, but in this instance I couldn't argue—in my eyes, Bob was number one!

A brother's courage, a broken match; what a difference two seemingly small things had made!

When North Winds Blow

"HEY, BOB, COME LOOK AT this," I called. We were walking home across country from our woodlot when I spied a curious disturbance of grass in a grove of pine trees. "What do you make of this?" I asked.

"Hmmm...Yeah, looks like something has been gathering grass," Bob agreed. "Let's scout around and see if we find an answer."

It didn't take long. I rounded a clump of birch and found where a big pine tree had uprooted. Beneath the tangle of roots was a hole, and there was no doubt that this was where the grass was going.

"Watch out!" Bob had come up behind me and now sounded alarmed.

"What is it, Bob?"

"It's a bear den, Gary. See, the bear has lined that hole with grass to keep it warm when it goes to sleep for the winter."

"Oh!" I jumped to my feet and looked all around us. There was no bear in sight. "Do you think the bear is already in the den?" I asked.

"I don't think so. Just wait a moment." Bob kneeled in front of the den and looked in. "No bear in there. I didn't really think so anyway. It wouldn't have left the door open, I'm sure."

"Just the same, I think we should get out of here. That bear might be angry if it found us fooling with its bedroom!"

We hurried home to tell Dad and Mom about our find. We had never seen anything like it before.

"You found a bear den, all right," Dad said.

"But why isn't the bear in it?" I asked.

"Well, it's like this," Dad grinned. "Have you boys finished splitting all those chunks of fir in the woodshed?"

"Well, not quite," Bob looked sheepish. "But we're working on it every day. We should have it all cut and piled before winter comes."

"Uh-huh," Dad was still grinning. "That's the reason your bear hasn't gone to sleep in his den yet. It's not quite cold enough. You see, a bear has to store up enough fat to last while it sleeps all winter. If it doesn't, it will die before spring. Probably it is still searching for food as well as getting its den ready."

"I can understand that, Dad," I replied thoughtfully. "There are so many different kinds of birds and wildlife around. I wonder how they cope with winter?"

"That's a good project for you and Bob to work on this winter. Keep your eyes and ears open and you will learn a lot. I'll give you a hint—they deal with winter in three different ways. Some go south for the winter to find the warmth they are accustomed to. Some sleep or hibernate for the winter, and some adapt themselves for the cold and snow."

"By the way," Dad went on, "even though some sleep through the winter like your bear, that's not true hibernation. The hibernators live in almost suspended animation. Their heartbeat and breathing slow down to the point where they are barely alive. Woodchucks, ground squirrels, snakes and frogs are examples of this."

"We've been hearing and seeing huge flocks of geese and cranes going over lately," Bob put in. "I guess they are an example of the ones who go south for the winter."

The Twilight Marsh

"You're right, Bob. They will go all the way to the southern States. Even hummingbirds do this. What's even more astounding is that Monarch butterflies do as well. They will fly all the way to Mexico."

For the next few weeks, Bob and I were especially careful to observe what was happening to wildlife in our area.

Two weeks later we went back to the bear den and found that the bear was asleep already. It had filled the opening of the entrance door with bundles of grass. We would have liked to explore a bit closer, but we had heard that sleeping bears are very angry if they are disturbed.

We had heard the term, *as busy as beavers*. One day we rode our horses to a beaver colony on one of the nearby creeks. Here we found signs of much activity.

"Look at all the stumps," I exclaimed. "They must have had a whole crew out here falling trees. I wonder where they stored the wood?"

"Dad says they cut the trees into lengths they can move and pull them into the water. See the trails down the bank?"

"Yeah, I can understand that, but I don't see where they put them?"

"I don't either," Bob said. "I guess we'll have to ask Dad about that one. Look, they've been working on their house, too, building it higher. Do you think that's to keep

80

it above the snow?"

"It wouldn't surprise me. Looks like they must be working hard to get ready for winter."

Dad knew the answers we were wanting. "Beaver harvest poplar and willows for winter. Both of these woods are very heavy. I'm not sure just how they do it, but beaver are able to pull these lengths of wood to the bottom and weigh them down with mud. In the winter they dig them up and take them to a place where they can eat."

"They want to make sure that their entrance tunnels are well below water..."

"Is that why they are building their house higher?" I asked.

"Partly, but there are other reasons. They want to make sure that their entrance tunnels are well below water, and that their feeding and sleeping platforms in the house are well above water. They strengthen the outside of their homes so that predators like coyotes and wolves can't dig into the living area."

"Wow!" Bob put in. "They must be awfully clever animals to know all that!"

Learning things like that made us watch even more carefully. We found that our horses and cows grew extra heavy coats of hair to keep them warm during the cold weather. Dad told us that this was true of all the animals that stayed awake during the winter, animals such as deer and moose, coyotes and wolves, and smaller animals like squirrels and mink.

We were coming in from the fields at dusk one night when we saw a covey of grouse fly by then dive into the snow.

"That's how they keep warm at night," Dad told us. "The snow insulates them from the cold. To prevent coyotes from finding them, they fly into the snow, rather than digging a hole while they are on the ground. After they are under the snow, they tunnel some distance from their entering point."

"I wonder what keeps them warm in the daytime?" I asked.

Dad had the answer for that, too. "If you could examine a grouse, you would see that in the autumn under each feather the grouse has grown a second one, soft and downy. It's like putting on a winter coat."

"How do they manage to get around when the snow is soft and deep?" Bob asked.

"Another marvel," Dad replied. "Grouse grow short tough hairs along both sides of their toes. It's almost like snowshoes. Lynx grow snowshoes, too, heavy, woolly fur around every toe. If you were to see the track of a lynx, you could mistake it for a cougar, its furry feet are so large."

One day we thought we had discovered a new type of rabbit. We were used to the snowshoe rabbits that were light brown, but the one we spotted now was snow white. If it hadn't hopped away from us we might not have even seen it. Finding something new was exciting. When we told Dad, he chuckled.

"What you saw is still a snowshoe rabbit. When winter comes, it grows a new coat that is as white as the snow. This gives it protection from its enemies, things like coyotes, lynx and owls. Some are still taken by these predators, but many more survive."

"Hey, that's camouflage, isn't it?" I said. "Do other

animals do the same thing?"

"Yes, weasels turn white in the winter, and there are several birds that do as well. If you keep your eyes open you may see flocks of snowbirds. They, too, are brown in the summer, but white in the winter. A ptarmigan, which belongs to the partridge family like a grouse, turns white in the winter, but it doesn't come down to our altitude."

It was Bob who noticed the next interesting example. We were out on our skis following a woodland trail when we saw a squirrel sitting on a log beside a large pile of pine cone shells. It was busily breaking open a cone with its sharp teeth.

"So that's where those cones went!" Bob exclaimed. "Remember last fall when we watched a squirrel dropping cones from a tree? It looks like they store them underground, then dig them out in the winter for food.

"I think you are right," I answered. "I thought they hibernated like ground squirrels, but they store up food for winter, too."

"Like we filled the root cellar with vegetables and our woodshed with wood," Bob went on.

"And Mom filled stone crocks with eggs in waterglass, and pounds of butter in salt water. You know what, Bob? We have to prepare ourselves for winter too, just like our wildlife neighbours."

The House Is On Fire!

IT WAS THE MIDDLE OF WINTER and ten below; it was time for tragedy to strike. I was ten years old!

I had no hint of what would take place that afternoon as I prepared lunch for Bob and me. Eggs sputtered in a skillet along with fried potatoes. Toast browned in the oven of our woodburning range. I put a mound of butter and blueberry jam on the table. Everything was ready when Bob burst through the kitchen door.

"THE HOUSE IS ON FIRE!"

The panic in Bob's voice sounded

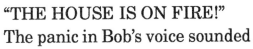

genuine, but I was used to his practical jokes.

"Who do you think you are kidding?" I grinned. "Come on, lunch is ready."

"No!" Bob shouted. "I'm not fooling, Gary! THE HOUSE IS ON FIRE!" Bob grabbed my arm and propelled me out the door. "Look!"

He wasn't fooling! Our ranch house was a two-storey log building with a steep, shingled roof. Even as we watched, small tongues of flame broke through the shingles and licked at the dry cedar.

It was coincidence that set the scene for the testing Bob and I faced that cold winter day. Dad had taken one sleigh and gone to the general store seventeen miles away. Mom and Uncle Charlie had gone to visit another neighbour who lived eight miles in the other direction. Bob and I had volunteered to stay home to do the chores. Now we faced the greatest challenge of our lives.

"What will we do?" I gasped. I felt the first grip of panic. If only Dad were home! Fortunately, Bob took charge.

"Get the ladder!" Bob shouted. He snatched up a bucket and ran for the water hole in the creek.

I dashed to the woodshed for the ladder. It wasn't there! I ran to the workshop. No ladder there, either.

"Never mind!" Bob shouted. "Climb up the corner of the porch. I'll give you a boost." Bob, one year older, took

control—how much older eleven was than ten!

I ran to the porch and scrambled to its roof. Bob climbed part way up and handed me a bucket of water, then raced away to fill another.

I had to claw my way up the edge of the roof proper with one hand while I carried the bucket with the other. At the top I had to walk five metres along the ridge to reach fire. Smoke and steam billowed up as I splashed the water down the roof. To my joy, the flames were almost extinguished.

When I reached my vantage point with a second bucket, however, I found that the fire had spread. This time the water did not smother all the flames. Worse still, smoke began to pour out from another spot on the roof below me.

I don't know how long we continued our frantic bucket brigade. My fingers were full of slivers while a catch in my side made me cry out with pain. Bob was ready to drop from exhaustion. My latest splash of water only sputtered as it hit the hungry flames.

"Hurry!" I shouted to Bob. "You've got to get more water!"

"It's no use," he said dully. "We can't put the fire out."

"Yes we can!" I screamed. "We've got to keep fighting!"

"It's no use, I tell you. Look!"

I was horrified by what I saw. Fire spurted up in half a

dozen places and spread rapidly. The place where I had stood to throw water was in flames. We had done our best, but our best was not enough. Still, the alternative was even more terrifying. "Just a few more buckets of water," I pleaded.

"No way!" Bob shot back. "Come down off that roof before I pull you down!"

Reluctantly I climbed down, the bitter taste of defeat in my mouth. "What do we do now?" I groaned.

"We can't save the house, but we can get some of the stuff out," Bob explained. He headed for the door.

What to get first? Blankets! We raced to the beds and snatched up as many blankets as we could carry, dragging them out into the yard, charging back for more.

By the time the beds were stripped, the fire had burned through the roof. Bob wouldn't let me go back upstairs.

What else would we need to survive? In the back of my mind I saw us moving into the loft of the barn.

Food! We dashed to the kitchen. Bob snatched up a box of bread and took it out to the yard. A large pan of milk caught my eye. Without remembering that our cows would give us all the fresh milk we could use, I picked up the pan and carried it out, not spilling a drop.

Dishes and silverware were next. Kettles and pans joined the heap in the snow out front. The crackling of flames above us grew even more frightening. We lost all

*Smoke and steam billowed up as I splashed
the water down the roof.*

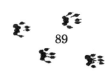

sense of order, snatching up whatever caught our eye. Finally we paused, gasping for breath, and gazed fearfully at the smoke billowing into the sky. The enormity of what was taking place overwhelmed us. All that we knew as home was being destroyed before our eyes!

Suddenly we knew we could take no more alone. Our small boy courage had come to an end. We turned our backs on the hideous scene and ran—ran until we could hear the crackling no more, until even the black smoke was hidden by the trees. We didn't look back. I was surprised to find that we were on the road to a neighbour whose home was three miles away.

"Maybe we can get help!" Bob gasped.

I nodded, too weary to comprehend that at this point nothing could help.

"Hey!" Bob exclaimed. "Where's your other boot?"

Startled, I looked down and saw that my left foot bore only a wool stocking. Then I remembered—waiting for Bob to bring water, I had jerked off my boot and filled it with snow to throw on the flames! It was somewhere on the burning roof!

A short time later we banged on our neighbour's door. We must have presented a sorry sight to Mrs. Galbraith when she opened the door. Our faces were covered with soot, streaked by tears. Our shirts and pants were soaked and frozen.

Quickly we gasped out our story. Could Mr. Galbraith come and help us fight the fire?

"Oh dear," she exclaimed. "My husband went to the store with your Dad, and so did Mr. Walker!"

Our hearts sank.

"Maybe...maybe we should be going back home," I stammered.

"No!" said Mrs. Galbraith. "You boys stay here and warm up. I'll get you some dry clothes. I'll get Mrs. Walker and see if there is anything we can do."

Left to ourselves, I felt the terror return and began to sob. Bob moved closer and put his arm around me. How good it was to have a big brother!

As time went by we became more and more anxious. What had started the fire? Were we to blame? We remembered another time, long ago when we were only three and four years old. Bob had found some matches and made a campfire—in the barn! We thought we had put it out, but the sparks ignited hay. The barn burned to the ground. Could we convince Mom and Dad that we had not caused this fire?

Dusk turned to darkness. We searched around and found a kerosene lamp, and felt better when the kitchen was bathed in its soft yellow glow.

Finally we heard the jingle of chains and the crunch

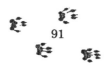

of sleigh runners on the snow. We dashed out the door. Mom was there. She swept us into her arms—not angry, just joyful that we were safe.

When everyone was there, we told our story from beginning to end.

"We're sorry we couldn't save the house," Bob concluded, near tears. "We did all we could, but it wasn't good enough!"

"I've smelled smoke for the last three nights!" Mom exclaimed.

"There was tar paper between the ceiling and the shingles," Dad remembered. "The chimney must have rusted through and sparks set the tar paper smouldering. That would explain why it broke out in several different places."

Our house was gone, burned to the ground with most of what we owned. It was an old house, however, and not very comfortable. With the help of neighbours, a new log home rose from the ashes of the old. People we had never heard of came forward to help. We had come from another country, strangers in a strange land, but now we had many new friends.

The burning of our home was a frightening experience for Bob and me, an experience we would not ever forget. We had survived our trial by fire. In the process, we stood a little taller, we had moved closer to being grown-ups.

More books for young readers from Polestar Press.

Dreamcatcher
by Meredy Maynard
1-896095-01-1 • $9.95 • Ages 10 to 16
A 13-year-old boy comes to terms with difficult changes in his life.

The Magpie Summer
by Judith Wright
0-919591-14-0 • $9.95 • Ages 12 to 18
A gritty, funny, coming-of-age novel about a 12-year-old girl in rural Saskatchewan.

Maybe you had to be there, by Duncan
by Sue Ann Alderson
0-919591-43-4 • $6.95 • ages 8 to 12
The zany antics and adventures of a 12-year-old and his best friend.

The Princess and the Sea-Bear and other Tsimshian Stories
by Joan Skogan
illustrated by Claudia Stewart
0-919591-54-X • $6.95 • Ages 8 to adult
Traditional legends from the Tsimshian people of B.C.'s rugged north coast.

The Snoring Log Mystery: Wilderness Adventures of a Young Naturalist
by Todd Lee
illustrated by Jim Brennan
0-919591-76-0 • $10.95 • Ages 6 to adult
Two brothers explore and discover the animals and habitats of their remote ranch home.

Starshine
by Ellen Schwartz
0-919591-24-8 • $8.95 • Ages 8 to 12
Starshine Bliss Shapiro tackles life's problems with the help of her hobby—spiders.

Starshine at Camp Crescent Moon
by Ellen Schwartz
0-919591-02-7 • $8.95 • Ages 8 to 12
Starshine's adventures continue as she heads to summer camp in pursuit of a rare spider.

Wanderer's First Summer
by Janice Erbach
0-919591-94-9 • $9.95 • Ages 8 to 12
A fantasy adventure story about young teens, telepathic sea creatures and a floating-island home.

The Whale's Way
by Heather Kellerhals-Stewart
0-919591-88-4 • $8.95 • Ages 6 to 12
A brainy goose and a teenage whale team up with two young humans for magical adventures.

Witch's Fang
by Heather Kellerhals-Stewart
0-919591-88-4 • $9.95 • Ages 10 to 16
Three teenagers risk their lives in this exciting mountain-climbing adventure.

These books are available from your local library or bookstore. For a complete catalogue of our books, featuring illustrated picture books, sports books, and the titles listed above, please write to:
Polestar Press Ltd., 1011 Commercial Drive, 2nd Floor
Vancouver, British Columbia, Canada   V5L 3X1